Learn to read with

Posy the Pig

Words by Sue Graves
Illustrations by Jan Smith

book-studio

"I'm going to a party!" said Posy the pig.

"I'll look like a pop star if I put on a wig."

The pink wig didn't fit. It was too big.

"I'm sure I'll find my green wig if I dig and dig."

The party
was held in
Sid Pig's rig.

For lunch, Posy ate a big, ripe fig.

Then, all the pigs danced to a band called Mig.

Posy won a prize for the best wig. She did a little jig.

"Wow!" said Posy. "What a super gig!"

The end